Published in the United States of America

By Steuben Press, Longmont, Colorado

ISBN: 978-1-7347800-0-0

Juvenile Nonfiction/Family/Children

06-2020

Momma, What Color Am I?

Joy Grimes Eke

illustrated by Nataliia Bielous

For Kelvin and Henry

"I praise you because I am

fearfully and wonderfully made."

Psalms 139:14

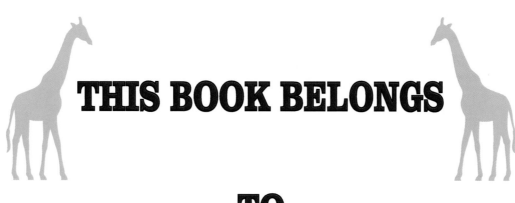

THIS BOOK BELONGS

TO

_____

Momma, what color am I?

You're the color of a

SURPRISE.

Life for you is a joyful celebration.
Filled with discoveries, new and inviting.

Tons of "Oohs" and "Ahs" about everything!
All things to you are fresh and exciting.

Momma, what color am I?

You're the color of

ROYALTY.

Your eyes sparkle like pearls,
precious and rare.

Your smile dazzles like diamonds,
nothing can compare.

Momma, what color am I?

You're the color of

HAPPINESS.

You fill the air
with giggling sounds.

And paint our home with
joy all year round.

Momma, what color am I?

You're the color of your great big

BEAR HUGS.

I love when you hold onto me
snuggly,

Your cuddles are the best,
sweet and lovely.

Momma, what color am I?

You're the color of

INNOCENCE.

The pureness of your face
brightens my days.

You warm my heart
with your trusting gaze.

Momma, what color am I?

You're the color of your

IMAGINATION.

A little explorer, who has many things
yet to learn and uncover.

Dream big dreams, dear One,
the world is yours to discover!

Momma, what color am I?
You're the color of

CUTENESS.

Your little face is the most precious by far,
You are a beautiful work of art.

A picture of you hangs on the door
of my heart.

Momma, what color am I?

You're the color of

SMARTNESS.

You are intelligent and amazing,
with a constant need to know, "Why?"

You have unlimited curiosity,
No one can satisfy.

Momma, what color am I?

You're the color of

MY LOVE.

Adored, cherished,
One-of-a-kind.

A treasure, a masterpiece,
You are a perfect design.

YOU ARE...

LOVED

POWERFUL

SMART

BEAUTIFUL

TALENTED

UNIQUE

CREATIVE

ROYAL

CHOSEN

"So God created man
in His own image;
in the image of God
He created him;
male and female He created them."

Genesis 1:27 NKJV

About the Illustrator

Nataliia Bielous is a native of the Ukraine, and is a professional illustrator.

Parents' Information

The author's purpose is to create inspirational content that celebrate and affirm young children.

To purchase additional books, and receive parenting insights, and affirmations for your child go to:

<u>forsuchisthekingdom.com</u>

Or

Amazon.com

Made in the USA
Middletown, DE
11 September 2020